THE
MARZIPAN
PIG

RUSSELL HOBAN

THE MARZIPAN PIG

Illustrated by
QUENTIN BLAKE

JONATHAN CAPE
THIRTY-TWO BEDFORD SQUARE LONDON

First published 1986
Text © 1986 by Russell Hoban
Illustrations © 1986 by Quentin Blake
Jonathan Cape Ltd, 32 Bedford Square, London WC1B 3EL

British Library Cataloguing in Publication Data

Hoban, Russell
The marzipan pig.
I. Title   2. Blake, Quentin
813'.54[F]   PZ7

ISBN 0-224-01687-3

Photoset by Rowland Phototypesetting (London) Ltd
30 Oval Road, London NW1
Printed in Great Britain by
BAS Printers Ltd
Over Wallop, Hampshire

There was nothing to be done for the marzipan pig.
He fell behind the sofa and that was that. No one
had seen him fall and no one knew where he was. He
shouted, "Help!" but no one heard him. Night
came, and morning, and there he still was.

"One would think they'd miss me," he said after a
day or two. "One would think they'd look for me."

Perhaps they missed him and perhaps they looked
for him but he was never found. Days passed and he
sweated as marzipan will. He grew swarthy with the

dust that settled on the glistening pinkness of him.

By day he listened to footsteps and voices that never came near him. Through the nights the street lamp shone outside the window and he waited in the dark behind the sofa listening to the ticking of the clock and the striking of the hours and the hooting of the owl on the common.

"There is," he said, "such sweetness in me!" No one heard him. He heard the rain beyond the window and the hiss of tyres on the street but no one came for him. Day after day he waited as the months went by. "I am growing hard," he said, "and

bitter. What a waste of me!"

One night he heard a gnawing sound behind the skirting board. "Help is coming," said the pig. He listened and he listened. Every night the gnawing sound came closer.

"Friends unknown to me have heard of my disappearance and are coming to the rescue," said the pig. "No doubt there'll be a big celebration when they find me. Crackers and party hats and probably a cake with pink icing. Perhaps I'll be stood on top of the cake and asked to make a speech."

He began to think of the speech he would make. "Dear friends," he said, "having spent long months in solitude behind the sofa, I speak to you tonight of . . ."

"Sweetness," said a voice behind him.

"Who's that?" said the pig.

It was a mouse. She was nibbling at him. "You're sweet," she said.

"There was a time when I was sweet," said the pig, "but I have known such . . ."

"Sweetness, sweetness, sweetness," murmured the mouse, and she ate him up entirely.

After eating the pig the mouse dozed for a time behind the sofa. When the clock struck three she woke up. "I wonder what that pig was going to say?" she said. "I couldn't stop eating him but now I wish I'd listened." In her were a craving and a sadness she had never known before.

"I'm so alone," she said. "It's so quiet here." She listened and she listened to the ticking of the clock. She watched the moving glimmer of the pendulum in the dim light from the street lamp. "Speak to me," she said to the clock, "do."

"Night," said the clock. "Only, only, only night."

"Surely there's more?" said the mouse.

"Lonely night," the clock said. "Lonely, lonely, lonely night."

"Ah! The loneliness!" the mouse said. "That's what the pig was going to say, I'm sure of it."

"Minutes, hours, days and years," the clock said.

"You have a kind face," said the mouse. "Make me happy! Love me, do!"

"Half-past three," said the clock, and went on ticking.

"You've more than that to say to me," said the mouse. She gnawed a little hole in the case of the clock and crept inside it so that she could be closer to the moving glimmer of the pendulum. She sat there listening to the ticking and the striking of the hours but the clock would tell her nothing but the time.

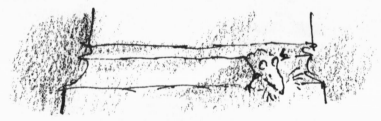

In the morning the mouse came out of the clock and went back behind the skirting board. But she came back that night and every night and sat inside the clock and waited for the clock to say it loved her. But the clock would tell her nothing but the time.

One night she didn't come back. The clock struck midnight and there was no mouse. Half-past twelve and one o'clock and still no mouse. While the lamp shone outside the window he struck all the hours and half-hours of the night but the mouse never came. The little warm place where she used to sit was cold and empty.

By day the clock could feel himself coiled tight inside and waiting for the night. By night he felt the empty place inside him as he waited for the day to come. The next time he was wound his spring broke and his ticking stopped and time went on without him.

The owl in the plane tree on the common was sitting where he always sat on Thursday nights, and it was raining. He was looking at the row of houses opposite the common when he saw a mouse come out from under the front door of No. 6.

The owl swooped down in silence through the rain and caught the mouse. He flew back up to the plane tree and ate the mouse, then he sat staring through the rain and he thought new thoughts.

"Love," said the owl. "Love, love, love!" he shouted to the rain. "I'm in love," he said more quietly. He looked down at the street and saw the violet glow of a taxi meter. Slowly the taxi puttered black and shining up the street, and in it was the meter violet-glowing in the dark.

"You!" said the owl. "I love you!"

On the taxi's roof the amber light lit up and said, "FOR HIRE."

"For ever!" said the owl. He swooped down on the taxi and landed on the bonnet with a thump. The bonnet was slippery with the rain, the owl slid on his tail till the windscreen stopped him.

When the driver saw the owl's feet staring at him he stopped the taxi and rolled down the window. The owl stood up and looked in at the meter. "I love you," he said.

"FOR HIRE," said the meter.

The taxi driver couldn't understand what the owl was saying. He thought the owl wanted to ride in the taxi. "I don't think you've got any money," he said.

"Who?" said the owl.

"You," said the driver. "Money. You know what money is?"

"Who?" said the owl.

"You," said the driver. "Money." He took a handful of coins from his pocket and showed them to the owl.

"Ooh," said the owl.

"That's money," said the driver. "No money, no ride." He started up the taxi and off he went. The owl flew up to the roof of the taxi and sat on top of the amber light.

The taxi driver drove to the cab stand by the Albert Bridge. The bridge was all lit up and shining in the rain. "Love!" said the owl. "Everything is bright for me!"

A lady came walking by. She was carrying a small handbag. The owl knew there was money in handbags. He swooped down and snatched it from her. He flew back to the taxi and dropped the bag on the bonnet. He looked in through the windscreen at the meter. "I love you," he said.

"FOR HIRE," said the meter.

"Stop, thief!" said the lady.

The driver gave the handbag back to the lady. He said to the owl, "You can't do that."

"Who?" said the owl.

"You," said the driver. "If you want a ride that badly, I'll give you one. But you'll have to pay me back some time, and not by stealing. Get in."

The driver opened the door and the owl perched on the back of the front seat by the meter. The driver started the meter and they drove off.

"I love you so much!" said the owl to the meter. "How much do you love me?"

"25p," said the meter.

"Love me more," said the owl.

"30p," said the meter.

"More and more!" said the owl.

"35p," said the meter. "40, 45."

"Yes," said the owl, "that's how it is. More and more and ever more. I am so happy with the lovely violet glow of you!"

"50p," said the meter as the cab pulled up at the cab stand by the bridge again. The driver stopped the taxi and turned off the lights. The meter went dark.

"Light up again," said the owl. "Tell me again how much you love me."

"That's it for tonight," said the driver. "Now it's time for trumpet practice."

"Who?" said the owl.

"Me," said the driver. He took a trumpet out of its case, climbed into the back seat, put his feet up on the back of the front seat, and began to play *When The Saints Come Marching In*.

"Speak to me," said the owl to the taxi meter. "Glow violet and lovely again."

The meter stayed dark and the driver kept playing his trumpet.

"This isn't fair," said the owl to the meter. "What have I done?" He jumped out of the taxi and danced with rage on the pavement. Without noticing it, he began to dance in time to the music. "What have I done, what have I done, what have I done to make you dark?" he hooted in time with the trumpet.

A man walking by threw 10p on the pavement by the owl.

"I want to see you glowing violet, I want to see your light again!" hooted the owl, still in time with the trumpet.

Another 10p dropped on the pavement.

"Nobody ever threw money before," said the driver. "You've got talent."

"Who?" said the owl.

"You," said the driver. "Keep singing and dancing. When you've made 50p you can have another ride."

"I want to see her glowing violet!" hooted the owl.

"That's it," said the driver. "Just carry on like that." And he went on playing his trumpet.

When the owl had 50p the driver started the taxi and the meter lit up again.

"Love!" said the owl. "You've come back to me!" And off they drove in the rain.

Under the plane tree where the owl had eaten the
mouse there grew up a little pink flower. A passing
bee noticed the flower and buzzed over to it. The
bee sipped a little of the nectar.

"Different," said the bee. "Interesting." It sipped a
little more. "Marzipan," it said. It sipped some
more, and grew a little dizzy. "I've been working
too hard," said the bee. "That's what it is." It
stopped buzzing and sat down to rest.

The day was warm, the breeze was mild, the
District Line trains rumbled past on the far side of
the common and the bee fell asleep.

When the bee woke up it was dark. The houses
standing opposite the common and the trains that
rumbled past it were all lit with golden windows.
The street lamps showed their globes of bluish light;
footsteps and shadowy figures passed on the
pavement. There was a full moon over the trees;
there was a smell of honey-suckle in the air.

The bee looked up at the moon. "No sun," said the bee. "I can't possibly find my way home without the sun to go by. I'll have to stay in town tonight."

The bee flew up over the street lamps and past the top-floor windows of the houses. At No. 6 a window was open, and the bee saw the face of a pinky-orange hibiscus looking round the edge of the window-frame.

The bee flew into the room and saw that the
hibiscus was growing out of a pot that stood on top
of a bookshelf about a foot and a half to one side of
the window. The stem of the plant leant to the
window and curved up gracefully so that the flower
could look out.

The bee flew round the flower and hovered in the darkness of the room, smelling the pinky-orange perfume of the hibiscus and looking at the light from the street lamp shining through her leaves and petals.

"Seen enough?" said the hibiscus.

"I'm sorry," said the bee. "I didn't mean to be rude." It flew round to the front where the flower could see it.

"You're not a gentleman, are you?" said the hibiscus.

"No," said the bee, "and I'm not a lady either. I'm just a worker."

"Never mind," said the hibiscus. "We can't all be posh."

"I might have been a Queen," said the bee.

"Oh yes," said the hibiscus, "and I might have been the Duchess of Gloucester but I'm not."

"You've gone to a lot of trouble to look out of that window," said the bee.

"That's not me, that's the plant," said the hibiscus. "The plant stays but the flowers come and go. Now I've had my turn. Tomorrow morning I'll be lying on the floor all crumpled like a dress thrown down after a dance."

The bee didn't say anything.

"At least I've got a full moon for my last night," said the hibiscus. "That's something. I wish I could have music." She began to hum in a high tinkly voice. "They play records here sometimes but they're out tonight. It's getting colder, isn't it?" She drew her thin and pinky-orange petals in a little. "So cold," she said, and wrapped her petals closer round her.

"I can't even sing for you," said the bee. "I can do a honey-dance though. Shall I dance for you?"

"Oh yes!" said the hibiscus. "Dance for me, do! Do it on the window sill so I can see you and the moon together."

"This is the dance that tells where the sweetest nectar is," the bee said. "It means, 'Sweet, sweet, so sweet! Sweet, sweet, this way!'"

"Sweet, sweet, so sweet!" murmured the hibiscus as the bee danced by the light of the street lamp and the trains rumbled past the common under the sinking moon. "Sweet, sweet, this way!"

As the bee danced it gave off the faintest scent of marzipan that mingled with the pinky-orange perfume of the hibiscus.

"Sweet, sweet!" whispered the hibiscus. She drew her petals tightly round her and drooped towards the sinking moon. "Fly away now for the honey," she said to the bee. "Fly so I can see you flying against the last of the yellow moon."

"I wish I could have been a gentleman for you," said the bee, and it flew off towards the golden passing windows of the District Line and the last of the yellow moon.

The upstairs mouse at No. 6 had watched the
hibiscus plant in the front bedroom for a long time.
She had seen the showy flowers one after another
bloom and shrivel and fall to the floor. She used to
sit behind the skirting board thinking how she
would go about it if she were a hibiscus flower.
Sometimes when there was no one in the bedroom
she would run out on to the carpet and strike
hibiscus poses in front of the full-length glass.

   "Poor silly things," she used to say to herself.
"They're pretty enough but they have no grasp. One
after another they make the same mistake: they let
go. The thing to do is, once you've bloomed, hold
on. Just simply hold on and don't let go. There one
is and there one stays. Yes," she said as she turned
round and round in front of the glass, "and I've
certainly got more of a figure than any of them,
though I say it myself."

One morning the mouse came out of the hole in the skirting board and saw a hibiscus flower lying crumpled and closed on the floor. For a few moments the mouse paced back and forth clasping and unclasping her paws. She stopped in front of the glass and looked at herself. "Today is the day," she said.

The mouse went to the sewing-basket and got a needle and thread. She stripped the pinky-orange petals from the crumpled hibiscus flower and out of them she made herself a stylish little frock.

"Chic," she said, turning round and round in front of the glass. "Either one has it or one hasn't."

"Now, then," said the mouse. She looked up at
the flower pot on top of the bookshelf. The graceful
curving stem of the plant leant out to the open
window and its leaves all quivered in the autumn
breeze.

The mouse climbed up the bookshelf and into the
flower pot. She carefully began to work her way up
the long curving stem of the hibiscus plant so that
she could take her place as a flower on the end of it.

"The thing to do is simply hold on," she said, but
the stem drooped and swayed with her weight, the
tight frock made her clumsy, she lost her grip and
fell out of the window.

The postman was just coming to the steps of
No. 6 when the mouse plummeted into his
post-bag. The postman already had the letters for
No. 6 in his hand. He hadn't seen the mouse fall into
the bag and he didn't put his hand into the bag until
he was coming down the steps.

When the mouse saw the postman's great big hand
coming at her she was very frightened. She bit his
finger, and not knowing what else to do, she kept
her teeth closed on the postman's finger and held on.

"Ow!" yelled the postman. He flung up his arm
and the mouse shot up into the air like a rocket.

The mouse flew through the air into the plane tree on the edge of the common. It was a Monday morning, and the owl in the plane tree was dozing where he always dozed on Monday mornings.

The mouse thudded into the owl and knocked him off the branch he was sitting on. "Oof!" said the owl as he went off the branch with his eyes still shut and his wings folded.

"Oof!" said the owl again as he hit the next branch ten feet down.

"Love!" shouted the owl as he grabbed the branch and opened his eyes. "Love has hit me like a thud in the stomach! Love, love, where are you? Who, who, who is it?"

He looked up and saw the mouse looking down at him. Not knowing what else to do, she was holding on to the branch the owl had fallen from.

"Love!" shouted the owl. "The breakfast of your eyes!" He meant to say "brightness".

The owl flew up
and the mouse ran
down the tree-trunk
as fast as she could,
across the street,
up the steps, under the door,

and into No. 6.

Once inside the front door
she stopped to
catch her breath.
"What a morning
this has been,"
she said.

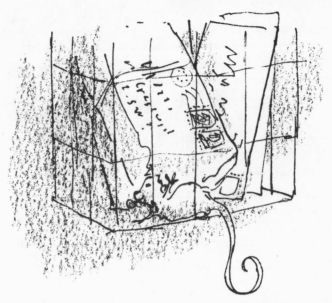

The mouse looked up at the letter basket on the door and saw among the letters a small brown-paper packet. She was very fond of brown-paper packets. "What harm can it do to look?" she said.

The mouse climbed up into the letter basket. "There's a corner of that packet just the least little bit torn open," she said. She sniffed the open corner and smelt something sweet. "It's not as if I opened it myself," she said, and began to nibble.

She nibbled her way into the packet and found a marzipan pig. "Lovely," said the mouse, and ate up the pig. The pig was fresh from the confectioner's and had no experience of life whatever. There was not a single thought in him, just marzipan. The mouse was tired from the morning's hurly-burly, and the sweetness made her drowsy. She fell asleep inside the brown-paper packet.

The little boy who lived at No. 6 came to the letter basket and saw the packet. That day was his birthday and the packet had his name on it. "Perhaps it's another marzipan pig from Aunt Constantia," he said. He saw the hole in one corner of the packet. "Perhaps someone's been here before me," he said.

He opened the packet. The tearing of the paper woke the mouse. She sprang out of the packet, leapt to the floor, and ran into the nearest hole in the skirting-board.

As the mouse sat there breathing hard, she heard the boy's mother call from the kitchen, "Any letters?"

"Three for you and one for Dad," said the boy, "and a mouse in a pink frock for me but she ran off."

"A mouse in a pink frock!" said his mother.

"Maybe she wanted to be a hibiscus," said the boy.

"Not any more," said the mouse as she sat behind the skirting-board. She did not take off her hibiscus-petal frock though. She went out that evening and did not get eaten by the owl. She was seen at three o'clock in the morning dancing on the Embankment by the Albert Bridge.